DARKSTAR
REBIRTH

UDDHAV

PARTRIDGE
A Penguin Random House Company

Back Cover Image: Man in the Dark by Zoroo (Deviant Art)

Print information available on the last page.

To order additional copies of this book, contact
Partridge India
000 800 10062 62
orders.india@partridgepublishing.com

www.partridgepublishing.com/india

For Satya, my best friend, Barnika, my constant companion in being a book worm and all my other friends from the 9th grade.

Love you guys.

Contents

Chapter 1   *The beginning* *1*

Chapter 2   *The Battle*..*7*

Chapter 3   *A way to defeat Divine Gwen* *11*

Chapter 4   *Mike Darkstar the WTS champion* *17*

Chapter 5   *The Rematch???*...*23*

Chapter 6   *Gwen seeks revenge*..*27*

Chapter 7   *A journey to...* *29*

Chapter 8   *Gwen finds the Diary of Lady Godstar* *33*

Chapter 9   *A couple of new members to the crew*........*37*

Chapter 10 *Oh! What a surprise!!* *43*

Chapter 11 *An apology and a warning*.........................*47*

Chapter 12 *A fight with Krum*..*51*

Chapter 13 *Krum's escape*...*55*

Chapter 14 *Spying on Krum*...*59*

Chapter 15 *Sam Godstar comes back with news*...........*61*

Chapter 16 *A shock*..*65*

Chapter 17 *Sriram's plan* *69*

Chapter 18 *A hideout*..*73*

Chapter 19 *Where has the vial gone???*..........................*75*

Chapter 20 *A surprise attack* *79*

Chapter 21 *Mike's night adventure* *83*

Chapter 22 *Trapped!!*...*89*

Chapter 23 *A battle of distraction???*............................*91*

Chapter 24 *Rebirth Of Lord*..*93*

Chapter 25 *Home and family* *99*

CHAPTER 1

The beginning

'Hey! Mike,' a girl called out. She got no answer.

'MIKE!' she yelled and she got a reply.

'Huh?'

'What happened?' she asked Mike. 'Your match with Rick. Answer me or …..' she closed her eyes and called upon her powers. She tried to read Mike's thoughts, and then burst out laughing at her own foolishness.

'Hey! Don't be so stubborn,' she chided. 'Tell me, did you win?'

Mike looked at the red haired short-girl in frustration. Her green eyes peered back with determination. Why couldn't she leave him alone? He wondered.

'Why?' he asked. 'Aren't your powers of Divination helping?' Mike scorned and threw a newspaper at her. The headlines were about their tournament. The World Talent Search Tournament in which people were made to fight each other one-on-one. The first heading was about her match. It said "Divine Gwen fights her way into the semi-finals." She was sick of that headline. She *was* proud of it but her name being the first name in the newspaper was a little over the top. She read on. The fourth heading said "Mike Darkstar crushes Rick Lava."

'You won, that's great! But then why are you so sad?' she asked, hoping it wasn't because she hadn't waited to see the result. She had been very hungry and did not wait to see if Mike won. She had gone to a nearby fast food centre and by the time she came back Mike's match had finished she had spent the past two and a half hours looking for him found him near the lake throwing stones into the water.

But Mike wasn't sad because of that he pointed to the draw of the tournament in the newspaper. Gwen saw that his next match was with Lord's friend, Krum's son, Arctic Armaldo. Lord had been a huge villain and had killed many people before he had been defeated by Mike's grandfather, Mars Godstar. Armaldo was the four time champion of the WTS Tournament.

Gwen half-heartedly tried to console Mike. 'Ah! Mike you shouldn't lose heart. Don't give up even before the match starts. You know what Alaster would say "tougher the opponent tougher you play."'

Mike didn't pay much attention towards her talk.

'Gwen, what weapon did you use?' Gwen was taken aback by such an out of the blue question. She clenched her fists and claws of iron grew from her knuckles. She then pulled out her small battle axe. Mike nodded like he was expecting this.

Then he asked her, 'How come we are the only ones who don't use magic?'

Gwen didn't want to point out that she *did* use seriously exhausting magic. Calling on the Divination power from her body to anticipate the opponents' moves *was* magic.

'What weapon did you use, Mike?' she asked. Then she felt silly Mike used only one weapon. A dagger his grandmother had made for him.

It was a twelve inch blade with a five inch hilt. The blade was made of a very special silver Mike's grandmother, Lady Godstar had discovered. Unfortunately she had managed to make only one weapon before she lost hobby-Mike's dagger. The blade was studded with diamonds which formed two vertical lines down the middle. He also had something else very powerful. His reflexes and his speed, unfortunately he could only reach the extreme of his speed when he was angry.

Just then a voice called out from behind 'Mike Darkstar, your opponent has conceded the match. You shall play your Finals next!'

****

The way Mike saw it, his father *was* right. Everything *did* have a bright side. He had been spending the last three hours throwing stones in the water thinking how long he would stand in the arena in his next day's battle. Then Gwen comes around to bug him even further, asking him what weapon he had used in battle, seriously? He had only one weapon!

Then comes his trainer Alaster and tells him "'Oh! you don't need to worry about your deadly opponent. You've already won.'"

But he couldn't stay excited for too long. His next match would be with Gwen. Mike was sure she would win the semi finals. Her semi final opponent was Giram. Even though Giram was twice Gwen's weight, he was stupid and easy to manipulate. Gwen had already defeated Giram thrice in a few other exhibition tournaments.

Gwen and Mike went back to the training centre where they could practice and improve their skills. Mike went to his favourite room, a chamber in which Ninja Blades made of rubber flew out of the wall and you had to dodge them. It was a chamber that tested one's reflexes.

As usual Mike took hardest level in which the blades came three at a time and at a very high speed. He practised for about half an hour and came out to find Gwen still in the Concentration room. She was glowing green. Mike was sure Gwen had lately been trying her best to read his mind. Fortunately for him he had learnt from his grandmother how to block his mind.

His thoughts trailed away. He thought about his grandfather. Mike didn't really remember his face or his voice. How had he defeated Lord? Mike thought. He was told many stories but he hardly believed any of them. But there *was* one story which Mike thought was likely. The story was that His grandfather had imprisoned Lord in some kind of a family heirloom supposedly a belt. But according to a prophecy "The Evil would escape thy prison" which could only mean… Suddenly he felt something around was wrong.

Then he realized Gwen was trying to read his mind and something told him she had succeeded. He looked towards the Concentration room and saw Gwen walking towards him, her face victorious. Before Mike could control himself his rage took over. The next second Gwen was on the floor. Mike had moved unbelievably fast like he did when he was angry and tied the laces of both Gwen's shoes and tripped her.

He was so angry he went out for a walk by the lake. After an hour or so he returned and found everyone in the dining hall watching television.

Now he knew why Armaldo had forfeited the tournament and had given Mike a walkover. "THE BATTLE" had begun.

CHAPTER 2

The Battle

Before Mike left for the World Talent Search Tournament his father had told him that he was going to gather an army to destroy Lord's remaining army. Supposedly their leader Krum was planning the rise of Lord. That was eight weeks ago. He had thought it would take at least a year to get such an army. Apparently there still *were* people who were ready to sacrifice their lives to weaken Lord when he rises, if he rises.

'I need to speak to dad' Mike told himself 'But how?' He had angered Gwen so she probably wouldn't help him. He looked towards her. She caught his eye and grinned. He ran over to her beaming.

'Hey, I-'

'I know' she said 'You want to talk to your father. I'll help you.'

'How did you know I needed to talk to dad?' he asked. 'Don't tell me you finally figured out a way to read my mind. That *would* suck.'

Gwen shook her head. 'No Mike, I didn't. I just felt you wanted to speak to your father, knowing he is going to battle. So, what message do you want me to give him?'

Mike sighed. 'Nothing, just ask him about the situation and tell him to kill Armaldo….You know Gwen? I still find the telespeaking you can do with my father completely unfair.' Gwen closed her eyes but Mike interrupted her, 'Gwen, ask my dad how Armaldo got there. And… all the best,' Gwen nodded and concentrated.

After ten minutes or so her eyes fluttered open and she cried out, 'He's been captured! Mike he's been captured!'

'What!' Mike exclaimed. 'What happened? Tell me everything, quick!'

Gwen started 'Your father was not at all surprised to see me. I asked him about the goings on. According to him the battle had begun last week. Your father's army had a hundred people and a thousand weapons. The enemy had twice as many people as your father and eight hundred weapons. He said the battle was almost over now. His army had over eighty three men and seven hundred weapons and the enemy had exactly eighteen men but their best. He said Armaldo went there with Krum's teleporter. Armaldo was one of the first casualties of the battle. Your father was telling me about some other danger when Krum hit him unconscious and dragged him away.'

Mike sat down and began laughing like a madman, 'That's it?' He asked 'My father is a tough one. He can easily break out.'

Gwen looked at him uncertainly. Then she continued, 'Mike, your father wanted to see you. So I showed him an image of yours in mind. When he saw your image he said he was impressed. He said you had changed a lot and were growing handsome. Rugged, tall, jet black eyes just like your grandfather's. But your father says you must cut that black hair of yours and also do more bench press.'

Mike snorted in disgust and said, 'My father is never happy with my physique.'

Just then there was an announcement. It announced 'Divine Gwen please report to the centre arena. Your match is about to begin. Your opponent Giram is ready.'

'Got to go,' Gwen said. 'And Mike your father asked me about your match with Rick. I told him whatever *you* told me.'

'O-o-o-okay!' said Mike.

'Bye' Gwen said and turned to leave when Mike called out, 'Gwen, all the best!'

'Thanks,' Gwen said and went in to beat up Giram.

CHAPTER 3

A way to defeat Divine Gwen

Gwen didn't know how to feel. Spectators weren't allowed to see any of the matches except the finals. Part of her was happy because then the next round opponent would not know your strategy and couldn't be prepared. But she was also angry because one couldn't show their skill unless they were in the finals, like only the best could show off. Gwen went in feeling confident she could win. As usual the match began with opponents shaking hands. Then a flag was attached to each of them on their back. Today's arena was volcanic type. They were given a radar that showed the opponent's location. They were then teleported away from each other.

Gwen saw on the radar that Giram was fast approaching. She got an idea. She saw a volcano and concentrated on it. She used her powers and saw that this volcano did not erupt. She climbed up and looked into it. Its base was considerably high. She jumped into it and saw that it was perfect. The opening of the volcano was only five and half feet from the base.

She looked at the radar and saw the blue mark that showed the opponents location was very close. She listened intently and heard footsteps. Few seconds later Giram's face appeared over the top. Gwen punched him in the face and pulled him down. She clenched her fists and her iron claws grew from her knuckles. Giram began to struggle, but with one clean sweep she cut off his flag. Then there was an announcement that declared her winner.

She ran out of the arena, grinning and found Mike. He was beaming at the results that were being displayed on the television in the dining room. He saw her coming and congratulated her. Then they decided to go and find Alaster.

They found him playing snooker with some other trainers who had come with their students. He saw them and gave Gwen a nod and gestured her to eat. While eating Mike began, 'Sooooo….'

She raised an eyebrow and asked 'Yeah?'

'This was your record seven minutes and thirty six seconds, *pretty* fast, huh?' Mike asked.

'Yes. He was an easy opponent. Strong but foolish,' she explained. 'So, what exactly happened in the arena?' asked Mike. Gwen began explaining everything, how she had decided to hide in a volcano and how had Giram stupidly stuck his head in to peep.

'He came straight to me almost like iron getting attracted to a magnet,' she finished.

On hearing this Mike got such a brilliant idea that he choked and fell out of his chair. 'Mike!' Gwen cried, 'Are you okay?'

'Yeah, yeah,' he replied 'I'm okay. Just choked up a little.' He finished his meal and went back to his room feeling very excited.

He had found a way to defeat Divine Gwen.

****

Mike went back to his room and was thankful to find all his roommates sleeping. These idiots had completely demolished the looks of the room. When his group had seen the rooms they were very impressed, now, Mike *himself* was afraid to go to the room because he might find something else broken or wrappers all over the floor.

Luckily, today Alaster had made all of them clean up the room and pay for all the damaged stuff. He hadn't made Mike pay a single zen, though.

Mike brought out his self invented tablet he called *Maaya* which meant illusion. It could work based on thoughts. He didn't need to tell or type anything all he had to do was, think about what he wanted and it would show on the screen. Even if he would get distracted and think of something else it would ask a confirmation message which was handy as Mike's thoughts wandered a lot.

He googled the world's most powerful natural magnets, the neodymium magnets found in most mechanical stuff like computers, radios and a million other things.

He knew a site that sold things like neodymium magnets and other things used in science. He ordered a fifty centimetre cube neodymium magnet weighing eight pounds. It was specialized by magicians to attract iron from very far depending on its weight.

The magnet, like most items, could be compressed. It looked like a like a dice until the side with one dot was pressed. Then it expanded into its original shape.

It was one thousand nine hundred and ninety nine xenix and ninety five zen in cost. If he wanted it to be delivered in speed post, which meant within a minute or so he would have to pay an extra hundred xenix.

He checked the amount he had in his bank account, eight hundred and fifty million xenix. He filled the delivery address and then clicked on the "buy" option below the picture of the neodymium magnet. He received a message that said that a transaction of one thousand nine hundred and ninety nine xenix and ninety five zen had been made from his account and his remaining balance was eight hundred and forty nine million, nine hundred and ninety eight thousand xenix and five zen. Then he received a message that said the selected item would be delivered in three days.

He opened a new window and closed the older ones. He checked out the radars used in the World Talent Search Tournament. He saw that these radars were used as pairs. Each radar emitted ultrasonic sound waves that were received by its pair. Each pair of radar gave out sound waves of different frequency, so the radar could detect only one radar other than itself, its pair.

Mike was now grinning ear to ear. Gwen might have had the power to predict the future but *he* had intelligence *change* the future. Next week, *he* was going to win.

CHAPTER 4

Mike Darkstar the WTS champion

He spent next week on magic shielding practise. He was very god at it now. He could block almost any kind of magic that tried to penetrate his mind. If the user of the magic was not full of confidence he could rebound it and then spell would affect the user.

He spent his spare time buying second hand neodymium magnets from the normal people. He'd figured out that magnets were cheaper in their currency.

Then he went around in the tournament orchards and collected a bunch of Abelia flowers. He went back to his room and was extracting the nectar and scent from the flowers when he was interrupted by Gwen; she had just come in without even knocking which startled Mike.

Mike tried to stand in front of the extracted scent and nectar. Gwen eyed him suspiciously but didn't question him.

'Alaster's calling you for dinner. He is unhappy that you didn't have any lunch,' she informed him. 'I'll be there in a minute.' Mike muttered and Gwen left.

When Mike entered the dining hall he saw Alaster was *not* very unhappy in fact when Mike entered he gave Mike a smile and beckoned him to call Gwen and join him at the table in the corner of the hall. He nodded and went to call Gwen.

He found her watching television. He told her that Alaster was calling her she nodded and they went to join Alaster.

'So,' Alaster began 'which one of you is going to make me proud?'

Both of them answered in unison. Gwen said, 'me!' and Mike said, 'both of us!' Alaster gave Mike a nod and Gwen a disapproving look. 'Don't worry,' he said 'both of you have already made me proud. I was just messing with you. So, did both of you prepare well for tomorrow's battle?' Mike nodded but Gwen only shrugged. They finished their dinner and went back to their room to sleep, leaving Alaster to play snooker.

The next day Mike woke up early which was unlike him. He went to the training centre to warm up before his match. He had two plans in mind but one of them had conditions of type of arena and it also felt a *little* mean. He'd use the other plan if necessary, but it was much more tiring.

After feeling he was ready he went to have breakfast. His match would begin in an hour. He went to the dining hall and saw that Gwen had already finished her meal and was talking to Alaster. He wished Alaster a good morning and sat to eat.

Just as he finished there was an announcement asking Mike and Gwen to get ready as there match would begin in another half hour. He went to the reporting room and told that he was ready. The tournament conductors asked him to wait in the pre-match room make any preparations if necessary.

He went to the room and, brought out the mixture of sweet smelling scent and nectar he had collected from the flowers and the spheres of second hand neodymium magnets he had bought. He sprayed the mixture over the magnets and put them inside. He waited a while longer then Gwen entered the room and flashed him a nervous grin. Then the referee came in told him to get ready as there match would begin as soon as the doors that lead to the arena opened, and even before he finished they opened.

The three of them went in and Mike was almost deafened by the cheering of the spectators. Gwen had been to finals twice before and acted calm. She waved to them and blew kisses to them.

The match began with them shaking hands. Then the flag was attached to each of them on their back. Today's arena was forest type and for some reason Mike seemed excited about something. The radar was given to them and then they got teleported.

Mike opened his eyes and found himself facing Gwen who seemed surprised too. The surroundings had changed which proved the teleportation had worked so that meant they were teleported to the same place *on purpose.*

He unsheathed his dagger and attacked at the same time Gwen decided to attack with her axe. He blocked her strikes easily but he could feel Gwen's power trying to go into his mind and anticipate his moves. With a bellow of rage he thickened the magical boundaries of his mind; the spell backfired on Gwen. Gwen fell down and her axe slid away.

Then she did something Mike didn't expect; she turned and fled. When she saw Mike running behind her and Gwen picked a higher pace. Finally Mike managed to get her trapped. There was a river ahead and Gwen didn't think she could swim after such an exhausting run so she turned to face him.

'You don't leave me a choice, Mike.' She said, 'Now I've got to use my strongest weapon,' she clenched her fists and claws grew from her knuckles. Mike chuckled. 'Oh! I have a weapon against them,' he said and brought out his neodymium magnets.

'Seriously?' she asked 'You're gonna throw stuff at me? Then … **BRING IT ON!!**' she bellowed and the crowd cheered. Mike made a big show of taking aim and threw the magnets, Gwen crouched to avoid them. She didn't expect him to throw all of them at once, and she definitely did *not* expect them to come towards her. All of them came and stuck to her claws.

She realized they were magnets and chided Mike, '*MAGNETS?!* What did you think, huh? These magnets shall stop me from attacking you? I must say, it would have startled me for a second if you had used them just as I was about to kill you. But now, you acted like a fool. How do you think these can help you?'

Mike just grinned, 'Wait and watch, Gwen,' he said.

She replied, 'Well, I'm *not* waiting Darkstar. I'm wining!' Then she charged towards him. Mike didn't even unsheathe his dagger. He just kept dodging only hoping *they* would hurry up.

A little later Mike glanced behind Gwen and suppressed a smile. He gave a slight cough and said, 'Gwen, meet my new friends!' Gwen turned and her heart filled with dread. Next second she was on the floor coughing.

He scent and nectar had attracted the butterflies in the forest, and butterflies carried pollen. Gwen was allergic to butterflies **and** pollen. Mike gave an apologetic smile to Gwen and came to take her flag. Then, he blacked out.

****

He woke up in the hospital, in a bed beside Gwen. He tried to remember what happened but couldn't. He was about to go out when voice called out, 'Mike Darkstar, your match was interrupted by a tear missile by a man known to be a criminal who was working under Lord. He has been caught.

'Your match has been rescheduled to the next week.'

Mike turned to look at the speaker. He hadn't ever seen him.

He asked, 'Who are you?'

The man replied, 'I am Andre, your new physician.'

CHAPTER 5

The Rematch???

Gwen couldn't believe how close Mike had come to defeating her. The plan Mike had used was pretty clever. She didn't at all think it was mean. *Anything fair to make you win* was kind of her motto. But she was scared of next week's match. It was announced that it would be on the forest arena *again*.

That evening she decided to go to the magical protection room. (*Not the one to which Mike went. Mike went for protection **from** magic, Gwen was going to the protection **with** magic room*)

She spent eight hours a day in the magical protection chamber and had a *little* progress.

On the day before their match Gwen realized she hadn't seen Mike since their match. She went to Alaster and asked where Mike was. Alaster told her he was in the technology room. She went to tech-room just when Mike was coming out.

They spoke while walking back to Alaster. Alaster told them they should go and sleep as their match was early next morning.

'Spectators aren't allowed for the match, but it will be telecasted on T.V.' he said. Both of them wish Alaster a good night went to sleep.

Next day both Mike and Gwen entered the arena a little late. Their faces were red with shame as they had overslept. Then the match began Gwen winked at Mike while shaking his hand, then they got their flags attached and prepared to be teleported Gwen prayed they didn't get teleported to the same place like last time.

When they got teleported Gwen checked the radar and saw Mike was very far. She looked for a good hiding place and found one. She hid behind two huge rocks. The place was perfect as she could see but couldn't be seen. After a while she checked the radar to see if Mike was approaching but was surprised to see the location of the blue marker that showed the opponent hadn't changed a bit instead it was in triangular shape showing she and Mike were at different heights She went in his direction, ready to play offence.

Meanwhile, Mike was digging a deep hole beside the tallest tree he had found. He went about a metre deep and realized Gwen was moving towards him. He put the radar in a polythene bag and dropped it into the pit. He refilled it and hid behind a boulder a few yards away. He had dug the hole deep enough to turn the opponents radar marker into a triangular shape.

After a few minutes Gwen appeared and as he expected looked up the tree as if she expected him to be up there. She began to climb the tree. Before she was halfway up she came down and to his surprise brought out her axe and began chopping the tree.

After an hour of exhausting work the tree fell. She searched the branches in confusion because she hadn't even heard a grunt from Mike. When she didn't find anything she sat down leaning against the rock behind which Mike was hiding.

She drank water and then threw her radar away in disgust as she thought it was not working.

From behind the rock Mike saw her throw the radar and did all he could to suppress his giggles. He could easily win now but wanted to take his time. Gwen didn't get up for a lot of time. Her energy was completely drained from all that chopping. After a little while she stood up and stretched.

'Now let's go find Mike,' she told herself. Just then Mike decided it was time he won and slowly crept from behind the rock and neatly sliced her flag from back.

Then he shouted '**Yes**! I win,' and ran around the arena whooping at the top of his voice.

Gwen couldn't take in what was happening. From where had this idiot come? If he was behind her why was the radar showing another location?

Before she could think of an answer he came and shook her hand. 'Well played, Gwen,' he said.

Gwen replied calmly though her insides were burning with anger, 'You played a clever game Mike. Congrats.'

Then a loud voice boomed 'And the winner of the WTS Tournament is .... *MIKE... DARKSTAR!*'

Chapter 6

Gwen seeks revenge

Gwen couldn't believe she had lost to Mike. She was a two time runner up and Mike? He was nothing. He was taking part in the tournament for the first time. She wanted to make Mike sad, or mad. She remembered Alaster kept records of his students. Points to improve and stuff like that. He also had close associations with Mike's father and grandfather.

She decided to sneak into Alaster's room while he was in Casino Indulge and search for anything about Mike.

That night she went to Alaster's room. She didn't have a torch or a lantern but that didn't matter the room had lights and she switched them on. She searched all the suitcases and trunks, she **had** found the record book but it didn't have much, so she kept looking.

She didn't find anything else so she decided to leave. Just then she saw a little briefcase under the bed. She opened it and saw it had a bunch of neatly arranged papers. She looked through a few of them then she sensed that someone was coming. She hastily stuffed the rest of the papers in her backpack and rushed out of the room she hid in the neighbouring corridor when Alaster came walking to the room, humming. She then bolted down the stairs and went towards her room.

She felt angry that she didn't find anything about Mike. She decided to look through the paper. She found most of them useless. She then saw the scroll she had dropped. She opened it and found a piece of paper inside it. She put it aside and studied the scroll. It was a map. The map wasn't very old. She then read the letter. It was addressed to Alaster. It said-

> *Dear Alaster,*
>
> *I have sent a map with this letter. It tells the way to my mother's diary. I want Mike to find the diary and uncover its secrets. Please don't give him the map before he turns fifteen. His birthday is on the 16th of February, two months away. Gift him the armour I made for his birthday.*
>
> *Yours Truly,*
> *Sam Godstar.*

Gwen couldn't believe her luck. She had hit *Jackpot*. She would go tomorrow and get the armour. She went to sleep happily.

The clock struck twelve, everyone was asleep. Unfortunately, Gwen had forgotten something. Mike's birthday was that very day. Mike turned 15.

CHAPTER 7

A journey to

Next morning Mike woke up and saw that a card had been pushed under the door. He picked it up and read it. It was from Alaster, a birthday card. 'Oh man!' He muttered, 'I forgot it is my birthday.'

He went down and found Alaster in a very solemn mood. As soon as he saw Mike his expression softened. He wished Mike a happy birthday and gifted him a shirt and trousers. Gwen seemed very sad about something. When he asked Alaster what the matter was he replied, 'Mike I am very sorry. Someone has stolen the map your father wanted to give you.'

Mike put a blank face and asked 'What map? Dad didn't tell me anything.' Alaster replied, 'Mike, your father gave it to me telling me to give it to you only after you turned fifteen. It gave the directions to your grandmother's diary.'

Mike smiled at Alaster and said, 'Alaster, I don't know what was in that diary and don't care either. The point is you have told me the truth. Thank you.' Alaster nodded sadly and went back to his room.

That afternoon Mike went to Alaster,

'I'm going,' he announced. 'Going south-east, to my dad.'

Alaster smiled at him and said, 'I was expecting this. You shan't go alone. Gwen, I and anyone else you want can come. You know, I find four the best for-'

'No!' Gwen interrupted. Mike was surprised to see her eyes were glowing green. Then the glow faded and she said, 'We shall be joined by someone on our way. Taking someone else could be dangerous.' Alaster replied, 'Gwen I don't care, it's a sentiment for me to have a quest with four people. *Anyway*, Mike-?'

'Stacy,' Mike said, 'if it's okay with her, of course.' He looked at Stacy expectantly; she nodded her approval and grinned at Mike. 'So it's decided, we'll begin this evening. Andre, take care of the others okay?' Andre nodded. Everyone went back to their rooms.

Gwen kept thinking why Mike had chosen Stacy. She was a blonde haired teenager with green eyes that looked like jade. Even Gwen's eyes were green but not like Stacy's. Her eyes were more leafy green. The only thing Stacy was good at in war was sword fighting. But her other talents like art and crafts were excellent.

The four of them met in the evening. They had to go about eight thousand four hundred and forty five miles. There only transport was the "Time Taxi" which according to Alaster would arrive at 7:30 pm which was a good time to leave.

'It can take us five thousand miles as it can't go out of the western hemisphere,' Alaster said. 'What kinda rule is that?' Mike protested. Alaster shrugged and told them the plan.

'Why don't we take a teleporter?' Gwen asked. Mike replied, 'Um, maybe because we don't have any. Even if we did we can't take any risks as we don't have a telepad on the other side where our teleporter can be received.'

Gwen went to a corner and thought for some time. According to Mike's father's map the diary was somewhere in London. May be she could get Alaster to stop there...

Just then Stacy spoke up, 'I've got friends in London who own a private plane. I'm sure they'll lend it to me.' Gwen took of advantage of that and said, 'That's good we can go till London in the time taxi and then leave in your friends' private plane to, uh what is that place?'

'18° North and 17°East.' Mike replied, 'Somewhere in south India. Hmm that's a nice idea Stacy. I think we should leave now, right Alaster?' Alaster nodded.

When they reached the taxi stand Gwen and Mike were surprised to see many different taxis. Alaster explained to them that they were all for different purposes but the time taxi was the best, fastest and the costliest, five thousand xenix per person.

As soon as Mike heard that he shouted, 'I'll pay!' He had received two hundred thousand xenix as prize money. He gave Alaster twenty thousand.

They put their luggage in their pockets after Alaster compressed them. Alaster spoke to the driver and told them all to get into the taxi. Gwen asked' 'Alaster how long will the journey take?' Alaster replied 'Three minutes.' Mike told Stacy, 'Hold tight.'

The driver pressed the green button near the steering wheel. Gwen shut her eyes tight expecting the taxi to go very fast but she opened her eyes when she heard Stacy gasp and couldn't believe her eyes. The taxi wasn't moving forward, it looked like the world was booming backward. She looked at Alaster and Mike they seemed to be enjoying it.

After a while the driver stamped the brake and everything froze. They got out of the vehicle. Alaster paid him and sent it back.

Alaster set his watch to England time and asked Stacy, 'So, where do your friends live? Do you know the way?' Stacy replied, 'Yes, I do. Let's go.'

They received a more than warm welcome at Stacy's friends, Daisy and Isabelle's house. 'So,' Daisy said, 'how come you're here. Do you want to stay with us?'

'Um, no.' Stacy replied, 'We need your help. We need to go to India and need to borrow your privet plane, if you don't mind that is.'

'No we don't mind a bit, but the problem is it has been sent for painting and shall return tomorrow. I am sorry.' Alaster replied, 'Oh, we can wait but uh, we need a place to stay and-'

'Second and third room on the left. Second floor.' Isabelle replied. They thanked her went to their rooms. Alaster and Mike stayed in one room while Gwen and Stacy shared the other.

Alaster went checked on Gwen and Stacy and saw them chatting. He told them to sleep and went back to his room and found Mike already asleep. He brought out a book and read for a while. Then he put it inside and he too went to sleep.

CHAPTER 8

Gwen finds the Diary of Lady Godstar

As soon as Gwen was sure Stacy was asleep she pulled out the map and examined it. Apparently she was **very** close to the diary. She tried to think where Mike's father would have hidden the diary. He would hide it in a place where everyone saw it but didn't realise.

She slowly sneaked out of the house to see if there were any libraries or book stores around. After a few minutes' search she came to a library that seemed right. 'Yes,' she thought to herself, 'tomorrow I'll come and check this library.' She searched a little more and then went back and slept.

Next morning she woke up at 9:00 am. She rushed down and saw that everyone was already awake. Alaster and Mike had gone to check on the aeroplanes. Stacy was in the kitchen talking to Isabelle. Daisy gave her breakfast which Gwen quickly gobbled. The she announced that she was going for a walk and would be back soon.

She went to the library that she had seen and saw it was open. She went in and looked at all the books in the ground floor. When she found nothing, she decided to go to the next floor. She was about to go up the stairs when she saw sign that said "NEXT LEVEL LIBRARY REMOVED AND SOLD TO GODSTAR ARTEFACTS."

She sighed and was about to leave when the word "GODSTAR" caught her eye. It was the name by which Mike's father had signed the letter. She dashed up the stairs and had a great surprise. The first artefact was a locket exactly like the one Mike wore.

She asked one of the workers where the manager was. He pointed to an old man. She went up to him and asked, 'These artefacts aren't real, are they?'

The old man shook his head and replied, 'No, they are copies. All of them, except that one.' He pointed to the book in the corner. The cover said "*THE DIARY OF LADY GODSTAR*"

'I want to buy that book. Give it to me, please.' She cried unable to conceal her excitement. The manager shook his head and said, 'It was given to me by Sam Godstar to keep it till his son comes to collect it.'

'I **am** Mike's friend. I have come here with him. He has gone out on some work and has sent me here. Please give it.' The manager replied, 'I want proof.'

'Okay then. I'll bring his father's letter and the map.' She said and went back.

She came back after some time with the map and the letter. She found that the manager wasn't there. She was about to leave when someone called out, 'Hey girl, look 'ere.' She turned and saw a crazy looking man. 'I'll sell you that crap for five xenix.' Gwen gave him the money and took the book.

She started back home, the diary in her coat pocket. By the time she reached it was lunch time. Mike and Alaster were back and full of cheer.

'We helped in painting the plane. We finished the job so fast the garage owner, Mr. Hick said he would give us a job and remove everyone else. We should leave after lunch. How much do you want me to pay for the plane, Daisy?' And without waiting for an answer passed a hundred and twenty five thousand xenix cheque for the international magic bank.

Mike went to the magic plane garage and spoke to the manager. The manager said, 'I think you should take Kevin. He is the best pilot in London. Though he's three weeks young to fly a plane I had him get an exclusive license at the age of sixteen. He is also very good in battle. He can accompany you everywhere you go.' Mike agreed to take this Kevin and paid Mr. Hick.

'Thank you Mr. Hick,' he said and left.

CHAPTER 9

A couple of new members to the crew

Kevin came just as they finished packing. He greeted them with a smile and gave Mike a fist bump. Mike immediately liked this guy.

'So,' he asked, 'shall we leave?' Alaster replied, 'Sure. Gwen, Stacy, sit with me in the back. Mike you sit with Kevin.'

Daisy and Stacy waved them a good bye. They all got in. Kevin announced, 'Everyone aboard! Fasten your seat belts. Flight takes off in 4..3..2..1' and then the flight took off.

'So, Kevin,' Mike said, 'Tell me about India. Where exactly are we going?'

'A city named Hyderabad, a very beautiful place. It has many legends. The world's costliest diamond the *Kohinoor* diamond was from Hyderabad. It was their pride before we, the Britishers took it away.'

'You seem to know a lot about the place.' Mike noted. Kevin sighed and replied, 'Yeah, I love that place. The new Hyderabad Airport is my favourite airport. I wish you could see it but we have to land in the old airport that is only for private planes. Though, our plane is um... unauthorized but I can manage."

After a while all of them had a meal from Kevin's green capsules. They had to think of what to eat and then put the capsule in water and whatever you think of is there.

After a while Kevin gave Mike a microphone and told him to announce that they would arrive in a short while. After announcing so, Mike looked out of the window and yelped like a puppy.

'Don't land here!' Mike cried. Kevin must have been used to abort landing on the last second because he did as told without hesitation.

Just then Alaster rushed in and stammered, 'Krum... and his men... maybe they know...'

'Cool down Alaster,' Kevin said, 'I'll land in those fields yonder.'

They landed in a football field and got out. 'I think we should rest here,' Kevin said. 'I have capsules that turn into rooms.' Kevin and Mike shared a room, Gwen and Stacy shared a room and Alaster slept alone.

****

Next morning they were surprised to see children rushing around. There room was surrounded by children in khaki uniform. One of them called out, 'You there! Are those rooms and the plane yours?'

'Yeah,' Mike replied. 'Uh, what is this place? We kind of had an emergency landing.'

'Oh! You are in the Hyderabad Public School and..' one began but was interrupted. 'Kevin, is that you?' someone asked. Kevin looked around and when he located the speaker he cried in delight, 'Sriram Ella! Long time no see. How's life?'

'I'm fine, my friend and, dude my name is Sriram Alla not Ella.'

'Yeah?' Kevin asked. 'Okay, sorry. Sriram, can you show us out of this place?' Sriram replied, 'Sure but our school shall start in forty minutes so I think hiding you is better. Come with me.'

They compressed their planes, turned their rooms back into capsules and followed him. Mike couldn't believe how big their school was.

'So, Kevin,' Sriram said. 'There's something important I need to tell you.' He looked at Kevin as if asking him if he could talk in front of these strangers. Kevin nodded.

'There has been a battle in our school,' he said. 'Not many people know of it, only a few of my friends who know of **our** magical world. The battle was underground quite near to **my** underground kingdom. I like to call the place **my kingdom** because I had discovered that place. Anyway there is a man locked-up in the place where the battle had been fought. I went there once when no one was around, he kept telling me to pass a mike message or something...'

'What!' Mike exclaimed. 'What else did he say?' Sriram replied, 'Um, nothing. I just came back.'

'Take me to him, NOW!' Mike shouted. 'Whoa, whoa wait. I went there a week ago. Then, there was no security, now there are hundreds of people.'

'No, no... not possible. Dad had told that there were only a few people left.' 'That's true,' Sriram said. 'Most of the people are natives who've been bought. People are ready to do anything for a good reward.'

Suddenly they heard footsteps. 'Shh,' Kevin whispered, 'Someone's coming.' They hid behind the bushes. Two men came walking by at first, their faces weren't seen but as they got clearer there were three collective gasps from Alaster, Gwen and Sriram.

Gwen and Alaster whispered in unison, 'Krum!' Then Sriram whispered, 'The other one is man friend's uncle.' Mike quietly unsheathed his dagger and prepared to pounce but Sriram held him down. 'Wait!' He said. Then he muttered something under his breath and sprinkled something on them. Immediately they froze.

'Unbelievable!' Alaster exclaimed. 'Water from the *fountain of frozen waters*. How did **you** get it?' Sriram replied, 'A gift from my friend. Well that's the end of it, though. Anyway, I know what to do with these guys, let's search them and rob them of anything that could strengthen them against you.' Everyone agreed and searched Krum's and the other man's pockets. Then they began moving forward again. Mike slowly went back towards Krum and his companion. According to Sriram the effect of the spell would wear off in a few minutes. Mike gazed at the belt which Krum was wearing. And for no particular reason he removed it from around Krum's waist and Krum's trousers fell to his ankles. He put the belt in his backpack and went to join the others.

Mike didn't have any idea why he had taken the belt. Maybe he thought it would be funny to see Krum holding up his trousers while walking. But he did not know it but he had taken the belt because it had a "G" on it. Every other member of his family had the surname Godstar. For some reason his grandfather had insisted that his surname should be Darkstar. This always made Mike sad making him feel like an outsider of their family. His thoughts were interrupted by a soft rustle of leaves ahead.

Again they hastened behind the bushes and on seeing the man's face again there were three gasps, from Mike, Gwen and Alaster. Suddenly Mike ran up to him shouting, 'Hey! Dad!' the man turned around in confusion. But on seeing Mike his expression changed to delight.

'Mike!' He cried. 'I knew you would come, what happened to your tournament?' Mike handed his father the trophy, or at least the compressed form of the trophy. His father beamed at him and asked, 'Uh, why are you alone?' When he saw the entire party coming out he gave them a smile and greeted them. 'Well, nice to meet you all. Mike I have something for you,' he gave Mike a writing pad. On it was written *Sneak Peak*. 'And yeah,' his father continued, 'I need to tell you something else... Bye.'

'What! Dad you can't just go.' His father sighed and said, 'I have to Mike. Alaster can teach you how to use the *Sneak Peak*. Now, I need to go to the airport. I need to fly somewhere safe. I think I should just buy an aeroplane as you know I can fly.'

'Then, Sir, I think these will be useful to you.' He passed thirteen capsules. 'The ten green ones are for food the two orange ones are for boosts of any plane and the white one is the plane.' He thanked Mike then left.

Sriram took them near a pond. He opened a trap door that was beautifully camouflaged. 'There are many rooms down there. You can use any room. Don't worry Stacy,' he said, 'this isn't the place where the battle was fought. Hmmm, it's getting late. I must go,' he said and left hastily.

CHAPTER 10

Oh! What a surprise!!

When Sriram came back in the evening all of them were busy. Alaster was teaching Kevin how to catch your opponent by surprise while duelling, Gwen was meditating and Mike was praising Stacy as she carved Mike's face out of a stone. He called them all together.

'So guys, what's the plan? I can move you out of here in the night. I've also booked a room for you at the hotel Vivanta which is right opposite our school,' he said

'Good!' Alaster said. 'I'll teach Mike how to use the *Sneak Peak*, till then.'

Within an hour Mike had learnt how to use the *Sneak Peak*. All he had to do was say "Darkstar Signing In" then he could talk to his father by thinking what message he wanted to send. And to close he had to say "Darkstar Over!"

They moved to the hotel after the sun set. After checking if they were comfortable Sriram left. Mike felt awkward because he had never stayed in a normal non enchanted place. Compared to the other places he had stayed in this place was a little too hi-fi.

They had dinner and then Mike thought about chatting with his father. When he brought out the *Sneak Peak* he saw that his father had left a message, 'Chat when you are free. Need to talk to you.'

He sent a message, 'Hey Dad, you there?' almost immediately he got a message.

'Mike! I want to talk you about something serious so don't do any other work while chatting, kay?'

'Right!'

'Good! Well the thing is, Krum has stolen the belt in which your grandfather had locked up Lord. So, I want you to find Krum and retrieve the belt.'

'Dad, can we send pictures through this thing?'

'Yes but I can't send you a picture of the belt as I have to be **looking** at the thing I want to send a picture of and then tap the screen.' Mike followed the instructions and sent the picture of the belt he had taken from Krum. He got a reply as fast as lightening.

'Mike, you awesome kid. When did you take it? Never mind, I don't need an answer. Just be little careful, do you see that case which is above the buckle? If you turn the belt you'll see a cartridge like thing. That is that's the prison for Lord's spirit. It is said that Lord had a blessing that he can only be killed under particular conditions. That's why dad, I mean your granddad could only defeat but not kill him. Don't ask me what the conditions were I don't know. A prophecy that your grandmother had issued tells them.'

Mike read that twice and then messaged, 'Dad, why were you running away today?' His father replied, 'Krum has placed a tracking charm on me. It takes a few days to wear off depending on the power of the charm. **I've** put a tracking charm on one of Krum's men just to know when they are close to me. Anyway Mike I've got to go. Learn well from the diary. Bye.' Mike immediately messaged, 'Dad, wait!' but the message didn't disappear from the screen, indicating the message hadn't been read.

He told the others about his conversation with his dad. Alaster and Gwen's face went red on the mention of the diary.

By 10 O' clock all of them were in bed. Alaster, Gwen and Kevin had set up magical boundaries for safety. All of them except Gwen slept peacefully. Gwen had a plan to carry out to night.

CHAPTER 11

An apology and a warning

In the middle of the night when Gwen was sure everyone was asleep she crept out of her bed and went near Mike's bed. She wanted to give the diary to him with an apology letter.

Unfortunately for her Mike had had Alaster to compress the suitcases for him and had put the suitcase somewhere. Gwen looked around for the compressed form of the suitcases. She finally found them in the drawer beside Mike's bed. She tried to bring them back to their original shape but in vain.

She got frustrated and put them back. Now, she had to give Mike the diary in person. She sighed and decided to do it in the morning. She wasn't going to tell him about why she had done it or about stealing the map and the letter. Then, she went to sleep.

When she woke up she saw that Kevin and Alaster were already awake. She went to Alaster and told him that she had found Mike's grandmother's diary and had kept it so long because she was angry and jealous of Mike. She asked him if he would train her control her anger. At first Alaster looked sad then he smiled and said, 'Sure Gwen, I'll teach you. Anyway, I was going to start the classes for Mike today.'

'Mike?' she asked. 'Why does Mike need anger controlling classes? Usually he is as cool as a cucumber. Even if gets angry it's an advantage to him. He moves like an electron when he loses his temper.'

'I know, but getting angry is never good. Mike gets supplied with more power as he gets angrier which isn't good. Anger causes destruction and if anyone gains more power as they get angrier...' he let it hang there.

A little later Mike woke up. Gwen gathered her courage and went to him. She handed him the diary and began reciting the lines she had been practising, 'I know I should have given it to you earlier. I bought it in an artefact store in England. I thought I'd gift it to you but I got greedy and tried to read it but couldn't. I repent my actions I'm sorry.'

Mike only half heard her. He had begun reading the diary. When he realised Gwen had stopped talking he put it aside and said, 'Gwen, you have done me a great favour by finding this diary. You couldn't read it because it is written in a script only my family can understand. It's hardwired to our brain. One of my ancestors had made this script. Anyway, thanks.'

Gwen was astonished. She wasn't expecting this. Before deciding how to react there was a knock on the door. It was Sriram. 'Sriram, how come you're so early.

It's just 10:30 am,' Gwen said. Sriram snorted, 'You Americans and your timings. In India early is before 6:30am.Anyway, Krum is using the airport as an entry and exit to our school as the airport and the school share a compound wall. At the main entrance there is too much security for them to enter.'

Gwen and Stacy asked simultaneously, 'How do **we** go to your school if the main entrance has high security and the airport entrance is being used by Krum.' Sriram rolled his eyes and said, 'You didn't think I'd be that foolish, did you? Come with me.'

He took them to the balcony. He went to the edge and dropped a marble. It did not fall down instead it rolled all the way into the school opposite.

Sriram grinned obviously pleased. 'I have made an invisible slope from here to the school, quite close to my kingdom.' The others were impressed they gave him pats on the back and high fives.

They went back in and Mike brought out his *Sneak Peak*. He saw that his message had been replaced by a message from his father. It said, 'Mike, Krum is coming towards your hotel. I'm in the school now but they don't know it as the charm has worn off.' Mike saw that the message had been sent thirty seconds ago. He immediately replied, 'Dad, the security can slow him till we leave.'

'No Mike, he's coming from the place where a marble came. He saw you through the binoculars. He's coming now.'

'Thanks dad, we'll take care of him.'

CHAPTER 12

A fight with Krum

Mike and the others decided not to go to the balcony. So, they looked through the window and saw Krum coming with five men. The bridge was only three metres broad so they walked one behind another.

Kevin pulled out a sword, went to the balcony and jumped on to the slope. Krum sent a man to kill Kevin. Kevin put his sword back and took out a rope that had hooks on both ends.

'I don't need a sword for you,' he said. He swung one end of the rope at that man. It caught him by the ankles. He struggled to free himself. Kevin swung the other end at Krum. Krum dodged and the hook caught the man behind Krum. Kevin pulled the rope from the middle and both the men fell over the opposite edges. Kevin cut the rope and both of them fell to their death.

Krum gave him a smug smile and sent another man. This man had a dozen daggers around his waist. He pulled two out and threw them at Kevin. Kevin hit one away with his sword and caught the other in just before it went into his face. He threw it back at the man's face.

The man moved to the right and the dagger went flying right at Krum.

Krum stretched out his right hand stopped the dagger in mid air. Then his hand began glowing red and the dagger melted into a puddle of metal and fell in front of him. Alaster yelled, 'Kevin, come back! You're exhausted.'

Kevin went back and collapsed on the bed. He woke a little later and saw that Gwen and Stacy had just returned after defeating the other two men and a failure with Krum. Alaster was sitting in the rocking chair having soda. Kevin knew that Alaster could defeat Krum easily but now he just wanted to see all their fighting skills away from practise.

Mike said that he himself had to defeat Krum and prepared to go. But to everyone's surprise he didn't unsheathe his dagger. Instead he took out a chunk of metal from his pocket and went out.

Krum saw him and smiled. 'Mike Godstar! At last I have the privilege to fight you.' Mike replied confidently, 'Grum, Krum, Rum, Bum or whatever your dung of a name is. You have the privilege to get lost before I... well I'm not gonna tell. And by the way I am not Mike Godstar, you goofhead, I am Mike **DARKSTAR**.' And he ran towards Krum with his full speed.

Krum raised sword to cut Mike in half but Mike was way too fast for him. He kicked Krum's sword out of his hand and locked Krum's ankle with his own and tripped him. He threw the chunk of iron at Krum's face. He knew Krum had the ability to melt particular metals with an out stretched arm or a touch. The chunk was too close for

Krum to stretch out his arm so it **hit** Krum's face and then melted. Krum exclaimed in surprise. This broke Krum's concentration and the iron turned solid right on Krum's face and Krum's movements froze, his concentration completely gone.

Kevin did a memory spell on Krum. Sriram then kicked him and Krum went skittering along the slope a long way before he fell of the side. Gwen looked at Sriram like he was an alien. 'Don't you worry,' Sriram said. 'He'll only break a few bones.'

Then, Sriram got rid of the bridge and said they were better off without it.

That evening Mike and Gwen practised anger controlling classes with Alaster. Alaster gave them two hours of lecture on how to control anger. He explained how we could save energy by controlling anger and use the energy for combat. Before they left he told them he would take a test for them tomorrow.

That night Sriram decided that his friends should see the city so he took them to a mall. They enjoyed a lot because none of the others except Kevin had been to a mall. They went to a 4D movie and the others came out complaining that they kept falling out of their seat.

Finally Alaster looked at his watch and said, 'It's almost eleven and the mall is still full of people. You people seem to have a much longer day than ours Come all of you let's go.'

Almost as soon as they entered the room the others fell asleep but Mike kept awake. He read his grandmother's diary. It taught how to make all kinds of magical weapons including really, *really* dark magic. Mike realized how dangerous a red book in a leather cover could be. He decided not to open it till was really necessary. He put it back in. He felt the suitcase was not a safe enough place for such a dangerous thing. If the diary fell in Krum's hands... it would be a matter of days before Lord rose. He decided to think of that later and went to sleep.

CHAPTER 13

Krum's escape

Next day Mike and Gwen were freaking out about the test. They went and prepared themselves before Alaster came. Alaster came in holding two small devices having two digital meters each. He connected one device to each of them with wires. He put two green wires to each hand two green wires and a red wire to the head. 'The red one gives you thoughts that anger you,' he explained.

He gave them a sponge ball and switched on the device. Instantly Mike's mind was filled with angry thoughts. He tried his best to control his anger. He took a look at the meters. One of his meters was at fifty and the other one kept changing between seven and eleven. One of Gwen's meters was at forty while the other was at twenty five.

Alaster turned the dial on remote in his hand in the direction of the "+" symbol. A sure sign of more angry thoughts. He held the ball so tight that it was wet with his sweat within minutes. Alaster slowly turned the dial again in the same direction. Even through the thoughts screaming in his mind he could here Gwen grinding her teeth.

The numbers on Mike's meter changed. One meter showed seventy seven while the other showed eighteen. Gwen's meters showed sixty five and fifty eight. Suddenly Gwen ripped her ball to pieces and threw it at Alaster with a scream. Both of her meters showed seventy. Mike resisted the urge to stuff the sponge down Alaster's throat. One of Mike's meters showed ninety while the other showed twenty one. Alaster switched off their devices and all of Mike's thoughts vanished.

Mike's heart hammered his ribs, he breathed heavily. 'So,' he said his voice no more than a whisper, 'did we pass or fail?'

'Pass?' Alaster asked his voice full of unmistakable scorn. 'You were awesome Mike! But um... nothing. By the way Gwen, you failed by a small margin but I can easily make you improve,' Gwen nodded weakly.

Gwen and Mike were shivering like dogs shaking away water after a swim so Alaster sent them to rest. When the others asked him what happened, he said "Overtime training!"

When she felt better Gwen got out of bed and joined the others. They played UNO, a card game for kids. Mike was still in bed and Alaster looked worried about him. She went to Alaster and asked, 'Why were you so worried about Mike after today's test, Alaster?'

Alaster said, 'Gwen, Mike has a very good ability to control his anger but he only pushes that anger deeper within him. If that anger was ever to come out all together... it would be much better for him to just get angry and let out his anger in instalments.'

'So, do you have a solution?' Gwen asked. Alaster nodded and said, 'But there is a problem. I can't read Mike's mind. Only three people can.' Gwen asked, 'Who?' feeling proud as she was sure Alaster would tell her name. Alaster replied, 'Lady Godstar, Mars Godstar and...' Gwen asked urgently, 'And who, Alaster?' Alaster glanced at Kevin.

'*Kevin?*' Gwen asked. This teenager being able to do something only two of the best magicians in the world could do... whoa!

When Mike woke up Alaster took him aside and told him everything. Mike agreed to let Alaster read his mind once in a while to remove Mike's anger from his mind.

After Sriram left Alaster went to spy on Krum for a while. Mike helped Kevin as he made capsules of food. Mike did all the non-magical work which was about 70% of the work. They made four capsules in an hour. Just then Alaster rushed in with a gloomy face.

'Krum's forming an army again. He already has eighty five people,' he announced.

Mike jumped to his feet. 'Where are they now?' he asked.

'He is at the airport preparing to go for something really important; at least that's what I heard him say.'

Mike thought a while and asked, 'Do you know where Krum's going?' Alaster nodded. 'Where?' Mike asked.

'*Sydney.*'

CHAPTER 14

Spying on Krum

'I'm going behind him,' Mike said. 'After all we can't let him cause any more trouble, someone must go behind him.' Everyone started protesting. Alaster said, 'I agree with Mike. Krum has caused us a bit too much trouble. We *must* send someone to follow him,' he smiled at Mike and said, '*I* shall go!'

Mike was about to protest when he saw that there was a message from his dad on *Sneak Peak*. It said, 'Mike, Krum's going to Sydney. I'm following him. Tell Alaster to join me at the airport at 8:30 pm. I forbid you from coming.'

When Alaster saw the message he said, 'I must leave *now*. Kevin come along, okay?' Kevin nodded and they went to get a cab. Alaster told Mike that Kevin could give him anger controlling traing.

The cab left and the others went back in. Sriram was staying with them for a few weeks. His family thought he was at his cousin's place. Kevin had told Mike that Sriram could do anything for Kevin because Kevin had once saved the life of Sriram and his brother.

Stacy asked Sriram if there was any training centre nearby. Sriram said there was one about a mile away.

Next morning they went there. Mike thought it was really awesome because it was the first training centre he had visited in which he didn't win in the speed room. Even in the WTST he had easily succeeded in the hardest stage.

After practise Sriram said he would give them a special Hyderabad dish called *Biryani*. After eating Mike drank a tankfull of water.

They visited the training centre every day. Mike hardly spoke to his father.

One day while Mike tried a lot to contact his father, Stacy called Mike and asked him to put away the *Sneak Peek* and join them as they played caroms.

While playing he got a message from his dad. He asked Gwen to read it out to him. She took one look and turned pale she showed the message to Mike.

It said, 'Danger around us! We were attacked. I am coming back tonight. Don't try to contact.'

CHAPTER 15

Sam Godstar comes back with news

'What do you think happened to send them back suddenly?' Stay asked. 'Not them. Only my dad's coming back because he said "I", remember?' Stacy asked why Alaster wasn't coming back. Mike shrugged.

'Well, whatever the case is,' said Kevin, 'We need to pick your dad up. I'll go to the reception and call for a taxi.'

When he went down he was surprised to see Mike's father arguing with the receptionist. 'Mr. Godstar?' he asked. 'Kevin!' Mike's father exclaimed 'Tell them I am with you.' Kevin nodded to the receptionist and Mike's father came along.

The others were surprised to see Kevin come back with Mike's father. Stacy asked him, 'Mr. Godstar you didn't tell us much. What *happened?*'

'My girl, I'll tell you everything but first, Mike, show me the belt.' Mike brought it out. His father examined it thoroughly nodding.

'Okay, now you want to know my story, right? Alaster and I arrived a little late in Sydney but we caught up with Krum. He went around the city as if looking for something special.

'One day he went to the *Opera House*. We expected him to go in but he went around it. When he went to a particularly powerful side, powerful like magical we could feel the magic around, he cupped his hands and chanted something. A few minutes later a vial fell into his hands. He then went back to the place he was staying. We were staying in a guest room adjacent to his place so as to spy on them.

That night Alaster said even from this far he could sense a lot of power in that vial, like being around my father or being around Lord. He said he thought the potion in that vial could regenerate Lord. We decided not to take a chance so that night I went to Krum's place and stole the vial. As I left a man saw me. I knocked him out cold but he could wake any time and arouse the house.

So, I and Alaster fled to the airport as we definitely couldn't defeat Krum's army. Ten minutes before boarding time Krum caught up with us and we had a fight. As the flight was about to leave I quickly ran, sat in the plane and came back. So, what about you? Have you been practising?'

'Yes dad we have but-'

'Have you been to the practice centre nearby? It's about a mile away-'

'We know dad but tell me something where is Alaster?'
His father looked down ignoring the question.

'Mike! I-'

'DAD! *Where is Alaster?*'

His father sighed and said, 'Mike, Alaster is *dead*!'

CHAPTER 16

A shock

Stacy couldn't help weeping. *How* could *Alaster* die? He was so tough, wasn't he? She wanted to kill Krum. She saw a tear roll down Gwen's cheek. Mike's face wore an expression of shock.

'Here.' Mike's father said giving Mike the vial of green potion. 'Alaster wanted you to have it.' Mike took it. As soon as the vial touched Mike's palm it began glowing. When the glow faded, in Mike's hand were two vials. One had blue potion and the other had yellow potion. Mike's father was astonished.

He said to Mike, 'Well, I don't know why that happened but keep them safe.' Mike nodded.

He had the yellow one compressed and he put it in his locket with the diary. He put the blue one in his suitcase.

A few days later Mike's father announced that he was going to get forces to form an army. Krum already had an army and could attack any time now. Krum was also very close to waking Lord. He needed the belt *and* the vial to regenerate Lord but luckily he never had both of them together.

That evening Mike's father called them all together and said, 'I have booked my tickets for tomorrow morning's flight. I want you to spy on Krum. Right now he is in New Delhi, India's capital. Book tickets for the earliest train possible. Okay, it's time for you to sleep.' Sriram told him that he could book the tickets for the next morning's train.

'That would be very helpful,' Mike's father said. 'I am glad we have someone to help us around here.'

Sriram went to the reception with his laptop. There was open Wi-Fi there. He booked the tickets, made a few calls and booked the tickets for the next morning.

He went back to the room and found everyone asleep. Mike for some reason had his shades on. Sriram locked the door and slept.

Mike wasn't actually asleep. He was wearing his *Google Glass* and watching Hindi films. He enjoyed these as they had loads of exaggerating scenes just like *his* life. After the movie ended he put the goggles aside and slept.

Next morning he woke up to Sriram's yelling, 'Wake up Mike! The time's 5:30 am. If we don't leave soon we'll miss the train.'

Mike quickly got ready and they left for the station. His father couldn't come because he had to catch a plane. They got into the train.

'Ugh!' Gwen exclaimed. 'This train's so untidy and the berths are so different.'

'It's awesome!' Mike said. 'It gives an adventurous feeling.' Kevin nodded. They spent some time talking. They had an early lunch and slept for a while. In the evening a man selling board games came by. They bought one and played for a while. At 9 O' clock Sriram said that they should sleep as their train would arrive early next morning.

Mike was the first to wake the next day. By the time the others woke up the train had arrived. They got off the train and took a taxi to a guest house. Sriram said that his uncle was a very rich man and could help them out. His uncle also could be trusted with anything.

That evening Sriram's uncle came to visit them. He asked Sriram if he wanted any help. Sriram said, 'We want you to find a man. His name is Krum he is somewhere in this city. Here's what he looks like.' He handed him Krum's portrait which Stacy had drawn.

'Sure,' said his uncle. 'I'll send my men.' And then he left.

After a few days, one evening one of Sriram's uncle's men came to their guest house and said, 'I saw this man near Qutb Minar. I recognized him from the portrait so I followed him. He was asking a rich man if he could hire a hundred and fifty men who have magical powers. The rich man lives in a white mansion three miles to the east from here.'

Mike patted him on the back and said, 'Thanks for the information. Here's your reward,' he said and handed him ten thousand rupees. After the man left Mike said to the others, 'Now that we know where to find Krum... *let the mission begin.*'

CHAPTER 17

Sriram's plan

They went to the white mansion and Sriram said, 'Here's the plan. I'm the only one whom Krum didn't see. So I think I'll join the group of one fifty men whom Krum's hiring and spy on them. Is the plan alright with all of you?' They nodded. Sriram gave them all a phone to contact each other.

He went in and knocked the door. An old man opened it. His face was wrinkled and his eyes had dark circles. 'What is it?' he asked in an irritated tone.

'Sir, I have heard that you were looking for magically specialized people for an army. So I just came to give my name.'

The old man looked surprised. 'I hadn't told anyone. Anyway come in.'

Sriram was lead to a big room with many people. 'My men, here's a new recruit the last one. Mr. Krum will be here any minute,' he looked relieved. After half an hour the door bell rang. Old men went to open the door and came back with Krum behind him.

Krum went around inspecting the men. When he came to Sriram he stopped and said, 'You are too young. We are going to a battle. We don't need weaklings like you.'

Sriram gave Krum a murderous look. 'I'm not weak,' he said. He drew his sword. 'You can check in fight.'

Krum smiled at him. 'Stand for a minute and you're in plus I'll give you double the pay. And that sword of yours, have a container ready to take it back. After all iron and steel, they are my specialty,' he said unsheathing his own sword.

Krum charged first. He went straight at Sriram's chest. Sriram bent and swung his blade in a huge arc. Krum had to dive aside to dodge the attack. Then, both of them charged at each other. Krum made many attempts to melt Sriram's sword but for some reason it stubbornly refused.

Krum pulled back looking irritated. When he saw the blade he was astonished. The blade which had looked like steel was now pure gold. Sriram grinned and said, 'Ever heard of plating? This is a sword made of gold, plated with steel.'

Krum scowled at the sword, then smiled at Sriram and announced, 'You are in the Lord's army. Be proud.'

Krum paid the old man thirty thousand xenix and gave the other men their share of two thousand five hundred xenix. He took his new army to an underground base in the outskirts of the city. They went in buses. Krum brought a whistle out of his pocket and blew it. Around thirty other men came from inside and joined them. He instructed these men to show the new recruits around.

After they looked around they assembled back at the same place. 'You have seen the place today,' Krum announced. 'From Monday onward all of you shall report here at 12 O' clock sharp. You've got come on Monday, Friday and Saturday,' He paused and looked at Sriam. 'Young though you are, you're great in combat. You will lead my army.' Sriam smiled and nodded.

Krum looked at the others, 'You can go now.'

Sriam messaged the others to meet him near the bakery near the white mansion. He had talking to do.

CHAPTER 18

A hideout

As soon as the others saw Sriram enter the bakery, they started popping questions at him.

'What happened?'

'Where did they take you?'

'Did Krum recognize you?'

Sriram gestured them to wait and told them everything. Just as he was finishing Mike cried out, 'There's message from my father.' He was holding *Sneak Peek*.

It said, 'Mike, are you spying on Krum?'

'Yes,' Mike replied and told him everything about their plan. His father asked him how many men Krum had. 'Roughly about two hundred,' he replied.

'God! There's a problem. We have only twenty men.' Mike replied saying, 'Dad, just take those twenty men and come along.' After a long pause his father said, 'Mike, I think you are right. I'll get these guys and come. Bye.'

All of them decided that they should start preparing for battle. Mike told them that they needed a base close to Krum's. It needed to be well hidden.

Sriram brought a map of the area where Krum had taken him. He showed it Mike. There were only three buildings around. A resort, a *dhaba* which is a restaurant kind of a thing and an apartment that had been demolished and was being made into a new one.

Gwen said that they could stay in the resort as it was the only place where people could stay. For some reason Mike looked very excited.

'Don't you see?' he asked. 'We could stay in the cellars of the demolished apartment.' Kevin slapped him on the back and said, 'You stole *my* idea!'

'So it's decided,' Sriram said. 'We'll go to the apartment. Let's go!'

They went to the apartment. They lost a lot of time excavating the way down to the cellar. They finally went in they were so exhausted they lay down and slept.

Mike woke up a little later and shook the others awake. "Hey, wake up!" They all got up. Mike told them that they should first have a meal. They went to the *dhaba* they had seen on the map. While they had lunch Gwen said she wasn't feeling well and wanted to go back to the base. Sriram had already finished so he went with her.

After lunch the others went back. When they came close to their new base they were shocked to see what was going on.

Sriram was fighting two men. One was in a red coat the other in green and Gwen's body was lying on the floor. Sriram hit one man in the face with his spear. He had recently changed his weapon because he felt more comfortable with the spear. He stabbed the other man in the back. He knelt down by Gwen's side as the other's ran to help.

CHAPTER 19

Where has the vial gone???

Gwen sat up in her bed. She was sweating and panting. Just then Sriram came in, saw that she was awake and told her that they were in a hospital far from their base. The doctor had said that she had fever and so must rest.

'I'm going out,' Gwen said. Sriram shook his head and replied, 'No, you must rest.' Gwen scorned, 'Oh please! Do you want me to break your nose?'

And without waiting for an answer she went out. She saw that Stacy and Kevin were talking to the doctor and Mike was frowning at the *Sneak Peek*.

Sriram came out and Mike saw them both. He didn't seem to care that Gwen was out of bed. He gathered them all together and said, 'My dad has arrived with 32 people. I told him the address to our base we should get back in time. Gwen, is it okay if leave now?' Gwen nodded so they paid the bill, thanked the doctor and started back to their base.

On returning they saw that Mike's father had already arrived. He smiled at Mike. 'They're safe, aren't they?' Mike nodded. He showed his father the belt and the yellow vial.

'The other one's inside,' he said and went to get it.

Sriram and Stacy stayed outside and spoke to Mike's father as Gwen and Kevin showed the others where to put their luggage. There was enough space.

'I was about to come with the twenty men like Mike had suggested but I met old Charlie. He said he could give me eleven more men who were hardwired for battle. Charlie couldn't-' Mike's father was interrupted by Mike.

'The... blue vial...,' Mike said. 'It's gone!'

'I knew it!' Mike's father said. 'That's why Krum looked happy. He is one step closer to Lord's regeneration.'

He shook his head as he saw Mike giving him the belt.

'Keep it,' he said. 'Your destiny is bonded with it.' Mike accepted this reluctantly.

Sriram left for Krum's base next day as he was asked to report. As soon as he left, the others started discussing about their battle plan.

Stacy drew a map of the area and on one side she drew an oval and wrote "*ENEMY*" Mike took the pen and gave positions to all of them.

'Kevin,' he said. 'I want you to lead the battle. My father shall go around the battlefield. I shall make a group of four people with me and attack from behind." Kevin nodded and asked, 'Whom will you take?'

Mike thought for a while and said, 'I'll take Sriram, Max and...'

'Me!' said a voice.

Everyone saw the speaker. It was young girl of about nineteen. Behind her were a dozen men.

'*LYNDA!*' Mike's father exclaimed. 'I thought you were on a quest to kill an army of *adeen,* the shadow monsters.'

'I got the message from my uncle and came immediately with my twelve *Naidaromer.*'

Mike's father grinned and said, 'Still didn't change that silly name. Anyway let me introduce you.'

'There must be at least one of my men every hundred square yards.'

'Okay,' Mike said. 'Listen to my plan. When Krum is in war it is unlikely he'll leave many people for defence of the base. So we fight our way in and I'll activate the hand-o-cap...' he shut his mouth with his hand.

'MIKE!' Kevin said. But he faltered under Mike's gaze and the matter blew over.

After their discussion Kevin went to Mike.

'Mike!-'

'Kevin, I know that you think the plan dangerous. But I have modified the hand-o-cap to explode when I trigger it and the trigger is portable-'

Just then there was a ring on the phone Sriram had given Mike. He picked it up.

'Hello?' he said.

'Mike,' said the urgent voice of Sriram. 'Krum's men are coming towards are base for an attack. It'll take me a while to come as Krum had sent me on an errand to the central part of the city. Prepare the others. Bye.' He hung up without a reply.

He looked at Kevin grimly. 'Warn the others,' Mike said. 'We have a battle coming.'

CHAPTER 20

A surprise attack

Mike didn't wait to answer Kevin's questions. He rushed away to warn the others.

Everyone rushed around, wearing armours and preparing weapons for battle. Mike snatched the binoculars from a guy. He saw Krum's army approaching.

Mike called for his to go to their assigned places. He cursed himself when he realized **he** leading the army instead of going to **his** assigned place.

'*CHARGE!*' Krum bellowed and his army fell upon Mike's. Mike ran straight towards Krum who had a smug smile as if he expected this.

His smile faltered when he defended himself from Mike's strikes. After tiring Krum a little Mike faked a shot at Krum's face and dropped his dagger. Krum raised his sword to protect his face. Mike caught the dagger in mid-air with his left hand and cut Krum's sword from the hilt.

Krum was surprised to find himself facing Mike with half a hilt. Mike jumped and kicked Krum in the chest with both his legs and Krum found himself flat on his back. Mike was about to finish him when he heard scream.

'HELP!' Stacy screamed. A man was standing over Stacy with his sword raised. Just as he brought down the sword Mike threw his dagger. It pierced him through the side of his neck and he dropped dead.

Mike walked towards Stacy. She was white with fear but she had a smile for some reason. Suddenly her eyes locked on something behind him.

'Duck!' she cried. Mike ducked just in time to hear a piercing sound pass above his head.

He turned and saw Krum with a sword he had probably picked up from a fallen soldier. Mike picked up a shield to defend himself. Krum just stretched out his hand and melted it. Mike had to drop it.

Krum came upon Mike in a full rage mood. Slashing, stabbing and making Mike feel glad that his reflexes were so fast. Krum hit him with the flat of the sword. Mike stopped the sword with an open palm. Next second he was on the floor from Krum's back kick.

Krum stood on Mike's ankles to make sure he didn't kick out and ruin Krum's plan of a perfect death for Mike. Mike closed his eyes. HE was prepared to die his army had crushed Krum's.

Suddenly there was a bellow of pain from Krum. Mike opened his eyes but wished he hadn't. A spear had stuck Krum firmly to the ground. It had come from the behind him and it stuck between Mike's legs, having Krum by the right calf.

Mike saw a few metres away who his saviour was. He saw the Sriram walking towards him, grinning. Mike forced his legs out and gave Sriram a fist bump.

Everyone else went towards Sriram asking him what kept him this long. Unfortunately, Krum's remaining army slipped away.

Mike quietened the others. 'So, what do we do with this guy?' Gwen asked.

'Let's kill'im,' Lynda said.

'No,' said Mike. 'Let's just take the vial first and think of what to do with him later.'

'Hey, Krum's gone!' Kevin cried out.

Mike went to where Krum was stuck. Now, the only thing there, was the spearhead. 'He must have cut the spear,' Mike said.

They went back to the base and faced an irritating problem. There wasn't enough room for all of them. So, Lynda took her group and with a few other people went to the resort.

That night, when everyone was asleep, Mike started preparing to execute his plan. He stuffed his backpack with his *Google Glass, Maaya,* a rope and a torch. He sheathed his dagger.

He wore a black full sleeved jersey, black trousers and black boots made of rubber. He was sure everyone had slept so he began his adventure.

He went out of the ruins cautiously and sighed.

'Krum!' he muttered. 'Here I come.'

CHAPTER 21

Mike's night adventure

Mike slowly crept down the staircase of Krum's base. He went in the direction Sriram told him Krum's room was.

He walked a little way and heard voices. He couldn't understand what they were saying so he moved into hearing distance.

'...yes sire,' said a high scared voice. 'I know it is bad news but our spy-'

'SHUT UP!' Krum bellowed. 'We can't rely on the spy for everything. The only bright side is that our enemy won't expect another attack so early. How long for the reinforcements to arrive?'

'They'll arrive here by tomorrow morning. We can launch a surprise attack by the afternoon.'

'Good! Now get some information from our spy.'

'Yes, sire.'

Outside Mike was listening intently. He heard footsteps coming in his direction. He hastened back to the turning.

He saw a short bald man walk past. He waited there and ate a bar of snickers he had brought along. A few minutes later the man came back.

'Sire, sire, a few of our men have arrived.'

Mike heard Krum's excited voice say, 'Come, let's welcome them.' And there was quite a bit of shuffling inside, which Mike realized, was Krum's leg. He decided to make a run for it. He was lucky Krum's earlier army had betrayed him in the battlefield and fled but if these so called reinforcements came now, he might get spotted easily and that would **not** be fun.

Mike made a dash towards the exit. As he ran out, he banged into someone. Immediately three men pounced on him.

He rolled aside to avoid them. 'Who are-' but the person never finished. Mike kicked him in the face and the man passed out cold, his face smeared with blood. The leader stepped forward.

'Are you my friend's son? What is your name?'

Mike decided to go with that. 'My name is Arctic Armaldo! Who are you to come spying at my dad's base?'

The man patted Mike on the back and said, 'I'm your father's friend. I've come with my men to help in the battle. So, where is Krum? I didn't see him in seven years.'

Mike waved his hand towards the base. The man nodded and said, 'A small group come within a few minutes. The remaining of my army will join us tomorrow.'

He turned and exclaimed, 'Ah! Here they come!'

He dragged Mike towards the group and said to the others, 'This is Armaldo, my friend's son.'

'No he is not!' one of them exclaimed. 'Armaldo is dead. He died in the battle at the hands Sam Godstar.'

Krum's friend looked at Mike as if he was a TNT explosive. Mike tried to make a run for it, but he was obstructed. Mike did a somersault over him. Just as the man turned Mike held one side of the top of his head and the other side of the chin and... Twist! Two down, twelve to go, he thought.

The other men were still in a shock. Their leader told three of them to attack. Mike kicked one, bent and kicked out in a huge arc at the other two. One of them fell down and made no attempt to stand again. The other one kicked Mike in the chest and Mike fell, groaning.

As the others closed up on him, he rolled between Krum's friend's legs and stabbed in the back.

'Aah!!' he cried. "That wasn't fair, stabbing in the back.'

'Fair?' Mike asked 'If we were playing fair, you wouldn't have sent three men to attack me at one time. I can defeat all of you if this was a fair game.' Krum's friend collapsed.

Mike felt something cold press against his throat. Before he could react somebody kicked the dagger out of his hand. With his speed he could register everything about the shoe which wasn't exactly useful.

'That,' said the voice of Krum, 'is precisely why I agree we shouldn't play fair.'

Mike tried to turn, but couldn't. Krum's knee held him in place. Krum stuffed a handkerchief in Mike's mouth and had him gagged.

'Powell, throw him into the box room and have my friend Ralph here, treated.' He turned to Mike. 'Don't wonder why I am not killing. That's in the hands of the Lord. You are the last in your legacy and-' he faltered as if he let out a secret.

The short man, Powell had two people throw him in a room after tying him up thoroughly. A little later he began to doze off. He was glad he could keep magic away from his mind. Judging from Krum's expression he would make attempts to read Mike's mind.

He woke up to the sound of the door knob. Krum walked in, went to Mike, removed his gag and said, 'Thank you, Darkstar!'

Before Mike could ask why, Krum stripped off Mike's jersey. Mike was about to treat Krum to a few magical words when he followed Krum's gaze towards his waist.

Mike couldn't believe his eyes; around his waist was the belt that imprisoned Lord. He was sure he had put it in his suitcase.

Krum saw his confused look and explained, 'The belt stays with its master or mistress until defeated fairly in battle. Even if you lose it, just think of it and it will appear within a few minutes.' Mike wondered how he was the master of the belt. Then he remembered his father saying that a family heirloom is passed on to the youngest member as soon as he or she comes of age. Another time Alaster had mentioned the belt as Mike's grandmother's creation.

'I want the belt,' Krum said. 'To raise Lord. Our spy has given us the blue potion. It can regenerate Lord's spirit. I'm sure you've guessed what the yellow one does. Thanks to you we've got the potions separated or *his* rise would interfere with Lord's glory.'

Before Mike could put his mind to work and process what Krum said, Krum came smiling towards him.

'Now for the belt.'

CHAPTER 22

Trapped!!

Mike's hopping, falling and rolling didn't stop Krum from taking the belt.

Luckily, Krum had forgotten to gag him. He went to his bag and pulled out the dagger with his mouth. For some reason, Powell had kept the dagger in his bag and then thrown the bag with Mike.

Just then, Krum rushed in his face red with rage. He hit Mike in the face and yelled, 'Where is the cartridge? What did you do to it?'

It took a while for Mike to process what Krum was saying. When he realized that the cartridge was gone he began giggling like a mad person, which enraged Krum even more. Before Krum could give him more violence, there was a knock on the door.

Krum went to open it, but before Krum could, the person on the other side opened the door and banged Krum on the face. The short man, Powell walked into the room full of excitement and then realized what he had done.

Krum yelled at him but Powell waved off the yells and said, 'Sire, I have excellent news. Our spy has managed to steal the cartridge. Tomorrow, when we attack we can take it from him.'

'Delayed another day!' muttered Krum. 'Tell him to keep it safe. I don't want any issues of losing the vial as it happened to these people." He glanced at Mike.

'**You** were the one who stole it,' Powell muttered.

They walked out of the room. Mike was glad they didn't see the dagger Mike had dropped. He picked it up and got back to his work of slicing.

He finally cut his wrists free and then the rest of the ropes.

He would prevent Lord's rise. He didn't care for the prophecy.

CHAPTER 23

A battle of distraction???

Early next morning Krum attacked the enemy base. Even his leg had been cured, mostly.

His army marched into the parking cellar. Suddenly, the enemy army charged, led by Kevin. They were prepared because, when they found Mike missing Kevin told Gwen to use her powers and fortunately saw the next day's danger.

Kevin was leading the army better then Mike had, and forced the enemy out of their base and into the open.

When Krum saw the panic Kevin had caused he took charge of the army himself. Kevin and Krum clashed swords. Krum began with offence right away. Their duel was so fierce that the battle around them seemed to have ceased.

Kevin understood Krum's pattern of fight and his weak defence. So, Kevin started on offence too.

Krum found it hard to face Kevin's attacks, so, he started taunting Kevin.

Kevin gave Krum the answer to each of his taunts. With a neat sweep he disarmed Krum. Just before he finished Krum him, chaos broke out behind him.

He turned and saw that Lynda and her men had arrived. Krum took the chance and slipped away.

They literally crushed Krum's remaining army. Without wasting time they assembled in their base to discuss Mike's disappearance.

'I'm sure Mike had gone spying at Krum and got caught,' said Kevin. 'One of Krum's taunts mentioned Mike and asked me if I wanted to know where he was.'

'That sounds like Mike anyway,' said Mike's father. 'So, do you think we should attack Krum's base?'

'We must be careful,' Sriram said. 'Today's a full moon night and Krum's sure to have an army of the full-moon monsters and *Adeen* ready to attack.'

'That's alright," Lynda said. 'We'll kill'em all.'

CHAPTER 24

Rebirth Of Lord

Krum had not fled from the battlefield because he was afraid he would die. Actually the entire battle was a distraction. After he had slipped away he had met the spy and had taken the cartridge.

He would secure the base with the army of full-moon monsters and the *Adeen.* But **he** would not stay in his base. He had some work to do.

He entered the base and Powell told him that he had cuffed Mike and the teleporter was ready.

Krum nodded in an absent minded way and told Powell to bring Mike. Ralph went to fetch him. He came back holding Mike by the hands and dragging him like a sack full of sand.

'DID YOU TORTURE HIM YOU IDIOT?' Krum bellowed.

'Ye... yes s... sire,' Powell said. 'Just a little. He had almost escaped, sire.'

'Do you want to give Lord a *dead* kid as prey?'

'I'm sorry sire,' he said meekly.

Krum went to the telepad and held Mike by the neck while Powell teleported them.

The teleportation brought Mike to consciousness. He was cuffed to an invisible wall. The place where he was, seemed very queer. Its landscape kept changing from a lush meadow to a bloody battlefield.

He looked around and saw Krum. Krum gave him an apologetic smile and said, 'Let's begin the ceremonies... with my master's magical staff.' He pulled out a long staff.

Krum turned his back on Mike and began muttering something that was **definitely** not a spell. Mike wiggled his right leg and removed the shoe a little.

'Not much of a ceremony,' Krum said. 'Just drop this liquid into this cartridge.' He slowly and carefully tipped the vial. Before the potion fell into the cartridge, a shoe hit Krum's hand. Krum dropped almost the entire potion. Only a few drops managed to get into the cartridge.

Krum turned towards Mike, his eyes mad with rage. He shot a spell at Mike with Lord's staff. It hit him in the arm and broke one of Mike's handcuffs.

'Do you realize what you've done?' he cried. 'You might have caused the biggest and most dangerous explosion ever. This entire island shall-' He was interrupted by a hissing sound from the cartridge.

'My master!' he said. 'He can save me. You have only delayed his rise. He'll rise in about half an hour and shall save me.'

'How long will the explosion take to occur?' Mike asked

'An hour at the most. I would have escaped with the teleporter if I had not destroyed it.'

As Krum muttered senselessly, Mike formulated a plan. Probably it wouldn't work but it was worth trying. He looked at the bushes behind Krum and gave a surprised look which Krum didn't miss.

'Dad?' Mike asked. Krum turned towards the bushes. He didn't see anyone.

'Your dad's dead now, Darkstar!' he said and sprinted in that direction just as Mike had expected.

With his free hand Mike pressed his locket, and it expanded into the vial with yellow potion. The belt had come back around Mike's waist just as Krum had said.

He knew what to do but still hesitated a little. Then he turned the belt and exposed the gap in which the cartridge. He uncorked the vial with his teeth, and poured the potion into the gap. He wiggled his wrist and looked at the time. Eleven minutes before Lord rose.

A little later Krum came back panting. 'Your dad may have found a good hiding place. But don't worry, when my master rises he'll finish your dad."

'Krum, how long would it have taken Lord to rise if the entire potion showed its effect?'

'Fourteen minutes,' Krum said. Mike sighed. He would have to survive for three minutes before he got any help, if his plan would work out.

A little later the cartridge on the floor started smoking. Within a few seconds, the smoke was so thick Mike couldn't see his own palm.

As the smoke cleared, Mike saw a handsome man standing where the cartridge previously was. Krum bent to his knees.

'Master!' he said, his voice full of glee. Mike's knees started to buckle. He was facing the most dangerous person of all time.

But the man seemed far from the mood of killing. He looked broken and kept shivering. A few seconds later when Lord seemed to have enough energy to speak, he looked at Krum and bellowed, 'Son of an Adeen! What have you done?' Krum pointed to the fallen potion and then nodded in Mike's direction.

On seeing Mike, Lord's eyes gleamed and a new energy coursed through his body.

'LEGACY OF GODSTAR!' Lord's voice boomed. 'You'll die at my hands now. And the prophecy-' Suddenly Mike's belt started smoking.

As the smoke cleared, in front of Mike stood... his grandfather? A bald and tall man. 'Grandfather?' he asked. The man turned and smiled at Mike.

He turned back to Lord. 'Lord!' he said. His voice was warm yet cold and distant.

'Mars Godstar!' Lord bellowed and just for a second Mike could see the fear in his eyes. He snatched his staff from Krum and sent a spell. Mike's grandfather swatted it away with his palm.

He made a gesture as if holding an invisible ball. A sphere of light formed between his palms. He blasted it at Lord. Lord and Krum jumped backward and the spell hit the ground and shook the entire island. It formed a huge cloud of dust.

Mike's grandfather turned towards Mike and broke his cuffs with a beam of light from his index and middle finger. He held Mike by the shoulder flew up. Mike realized they were standing on a nimbus.

Below them the island exploded. Mike was about to ask his grandfather what would happen to Lord after *that* explosion.

His grandfather answered him first. 'They escaped. I saw Lord go I the other direction. He **had** to flee because he did not have the power to face me. Anyway, where do we go?'

Mike told him, his grandfather nodded and flew faster.

Mike was delighted. He was going back home... with the greatest magician ever.

CHAPTER 25

Home and family

Kevin was disgusted. He had formed an excellent army and had led the assault. He had taken on at least a hundred and eighty full-moon monsters and twice as many Adeen with his small group, compared to the enemy.

He went to Sriram who was fighting an Adeen. Whenever Sriram tried to speak the Adeen blasted a shadow ball at him. Kevin got frustrated and cut it in half.

'Sriram, let's go and find Mike. Our men can handle these things.'

'Right! Let's go,' said Sriram and they ran in. They looked everywhere but didn't find Mike.

When they came to what looked like the control room they heard someone laughing.

'Listen,' Sriram said. 'I'll go and tackle whoever is inside.' But before **Sriram** could protest, **Kevin** sprinted in.

When Powell saw Kevin coming in he said, 'Gone! He's gone! Krum took him.' Kevin had enough senseless talk for one day. He slashed his sword across Powell's neck and killed him.

They went out and were surprised to see that the battle had ended. They told everyone the weird man's words.

'Let's go back and talk about it,' said Mike's father grimly. Mike's father went ahead of the others with Lynda and her group.

As Kevin's group neared the base everyone pointed up and gasped. Kevin looked up in disbelief as Mike and an old man came flying down, on a cloud.

Mike was grinning at all of them. Their cloud landed right in the middle of the group. As many parted to make space, one ran forward.

Stacy ran to Mike and hugged him. 'You're **not** going like that again.' She shouted on his face.

Mike grinned. 'Yes ma'am,' he said. Suddenly he surged forward and kissed her. He expected her to pull back and punch him in the face, but she didn't make any sign of protest.

Mike realized everyone was watching and heard a cough from Kevin. They pulled back their faces red as tomatoes.

'So, anyway,' Mike said. 'The thing is...'

'Lord has risen and so have I,' finished the old man. There was a collective gasp from the group.

'Who,' Sriram asked. 'Are you?'

'Uh, Sriram.' Mike said 'This,' Mike glanced at his grandfather. 'Is my.... grandfather, MARS GODSTAR!'